THE GENERAL'S SECRET

DEDICATION

To Hazel Patton, the woman who inspired Salem's Riverfront Carousel. To my mother who made me believe anything is possible. And to my children, stepchildren, their partners, and all of my grandkids because every one of them is uniquely and exquisitely human, and each holds a special place in my heart.

Special thanks to the people who made generous
donations to help finance the publication of this book:

Edward H. and Ann Allen, the Carousel's *Horse's Mouth Sponsors*.
Hazel Patton's family, Sara, Matthew, Mike, Jim, Charles, Rob, Bill, their spouses
and children because they feel Hazel and Roy bring out the best in all of them.
Beautiful America Publishing Company
The West Salem and The Capitol Lions Clubs.

Published by
Little America Publishing Company
(an imprint of Beautiful America Publishing Company)
P.O. Box 244, 2600 Progress Way
Woodburn, OR 97071

Library of Congress Catalog Number 2001029889
ISBN 0-89802-758-6

The General's Secret

By Elaine K. Sanchez
Illustrated by Janee Hughes

Something was terribly wrong with the Carousel. The horses were behaving very badly. Every horse wanted to be first, but since the Carousel went around in circles, no one knew where FIRST was. So every horse was trying to outrun every other horse, and there was a lot of bumping and shoving going on. West Wind had tried to pass Brown Beauty and somehow they'd tripped Rosinante, and that was the beginning of the pile up.

Dave, the head carver, had been patient at first, but now he was angry. He stood on the platform, hands on his skinny hips, looking totally frustrated as he faced the tangle of legs, manes, and tails before him. "This horsin' around has gone too far. Racing and pushing is dangerous. Someone is going to get hurt. You are behaving like fools!"

Little Joe started to cry. "What's wrong with being a foal?"
Bucky snorted and said gruffly, "He said fool, not foal. Stop crying. You're acting like a baby."

"I am a baby."
"Well, you don't have to act like one."
"I don't know how to act like anything else. This is how they carved me."
Bucky threw his head forward, and WHACK! He smacked the center panel with both hind hooves.

"Bucky!" hollered Dave. "Stop that right now. You're going to break something."

"He's always doing that," tattled Heather, the dainty little horse with the ruffle of lace peeking out from under her shiny red saddle.

"Bucky's my name, and I was made to buck. That's my job, so leave me alone and stay out of the way." He kicked again, and this time he connected with Cloudwalker, putting a terrible gash in the horse's right fetlock.

Cloudwalker fell to the platform. "Ow! Ow! Ow!" he cried. "Oh, you poor thing. That looks terrible. Is it broken?" gasped Big Sky, the horse with a heart as big as Montana.

"If it is, it's his own fault," grumbled Sarah Jane. "He's always looking up at the sky instead of paying attention to what's going on right in front of him."

7

"Sarah Jane, you're just an old hag," accused Rain Dancer.

"Young man, I was named for a nine-year-old girl who came across America on the Oregon Trail a hundred and fifty years ago, and she was a lot tougher than you are. I'm proud of the pioneer spirit that was carved into me; so you can just take your cloud and go rain on someone else's parade." Sarah Jane pushed her way past Rain Dancer swishing her tail and slapping him sharply across the nose.

Rain Dancer's eyes misted so heavily from the sting of Sarah Jane's tail that his tears made the platform wet and slippery.

"Just like him," whispered Bondo. "He calls other horses names, but when someone says something mean to him, he clouds up and cries all over everything."

Magic spoke up. "Stop arguing–all of you. Dave is right. We are acting badly. Let's choose a leader and come up with some rules we can all live by."

"Oh, what would you know, Magic?" snorted Legal Tender. "Your mother was a board."

Rosinante spoke up. "So what if his mother was a board. All of us started out as trees."

"I didn't mean that kind of board. Magic was adopted by the board of directors," replied Legal Tender.

"So?" asked Rosinante.

"So, what can he know about anything? He's had so much input from so many people that he has at least fourteen different opinions on any given subject."

Magic stuck his horn up high in the air. "Yeah, and you were adopted by a bank. You probably think it's money that makes the Carousel go around."

No one really remembered the final insult that started the next fight, and it was impossible to tell who bit whom first. But it was a terrible mess. There were chips in teeth, scratches in paint, and at least four horses were missing chunks of hair from their manes and tails when it was over.

After Dave broke it up and saw the damage the horses had done to each other he stood before them and said, "I am so disappointed in the way you have behaved. Do you have any idea how many people have loved you since you were just blocks of wood? What are the carvers and painters going to think? And what about the children? Did any of you stop to think about the example you're setting?"

All the horses hung their heads. Even those who hadn't been involved in the fight felt badly for what had happened. They especially felt sad that they had let Dave down.

Magic flapped his wings, trying to straighten out a couple of bent feathers. "I know I brought this up earlier, and I'm sure Legal Tender will be surprised to hear that my opinion hasn't changed, but the truth is we need a leader. And I was thinking, since Dave is the master carver, maybe it should be his horse, Morning Glory."

"Well, she is beautiful, and a very nice horse," said Rain Dancer, wiping his eyes on Kate's quilted saddle blanket, but I don't think she'd be a good leader."

"Why wouldn't I?" asked Morning Glory sounding a little hurt.

"You start the day out great, but you get a little droopy in the late afternoon."

Morning Glory sighed, "You're right; I do. Well, then, how about Francis?"

Cloudwalker, who had gotten a splinter in his tongue while licking the wound on his leg sounded a little grumpy when he said, "No way. He won't go anywhere without Kate. Haven't you seen the way he's always winking at her? Besides, he's too stubborn to be a good leader."

"Good point," West Wind muttered. "What about Jazz or Highland Laddie?"

"Jazz is from Africa. He likes beating drums and complicated rhythms. He might do away with our organ. And Highland Laddie's from Scotland. He'd probably make us wear kilts and listen to bagpipe music."

They all looked at each other. Surely there was one of them that could take charge.

Heather pranced excitedly. "Listen to me, everyone! Listen! We've all overlooked the most obvious choice—The General. He's a big, proud horse. I think he was named for the famous General Patton in World War II. Look at his flag. He's perfect."

"I'm not so sure he was named after that general. Besides, I've never heard him utter so much as a whinny," said Thunder, the school children's horse.

Abbie nudged Goldie and whispered, "I've always liked the strong, silent type." They both giggled.

"I heard he has a secret," said Sarah Jane.

"What kind of a secret?" asked Seahorse Dawn.

"I don't know, but if he really was named for General George S. Patton, I bet he says bad words, and you can't be a Carousel horse and cuss in front of kids," said Snickerdoodle.

Everyone knew that a horse would get kicked off the Carousel for saying bad words—no questions asked.

"Well, if he's that kind of a horse, he should keep his mouth shut, and we should all avoid him," suggested Tropical Breeze.

"Let's not fight any more," said the Peace Pony. "Let's talk to him and tell him we understand his problem, and that we'll help him overcome it. We'll explain that we all want to get along, but we need someone strong, and brave, and smart to be in charge."

Ruby Rose suggested Woodland's Crusader should approach The General. "Woodland's Crusader has all that fancy armor and three shields on his side. The General will know we've sent someone important to ask him. What do you think?"

The horses looked from one to another. For once they finally agreed on something.

Woodland's Crusader marched up to The General, cleared his throat, then said, "Excuse me, General, sir. The horses of Salem's Riverfront Carousel have decided we would like you to be our leader."

The General smiled, but didn't say anything.

Woodland's Crusader continued, "We think we understand your silence. We figured your secret is – you know – the bad words. There are certain things you just can't say on the Carousel. You understand that, don't you sir?"

He nodded.

"Well, then, it's settled. You are the right horse to help us. Will you be our leader?"

The General looked thoughtful and waited a few moments before replying. Finally, when everyone was quiet and paying absolute attention, The General gave his answer.

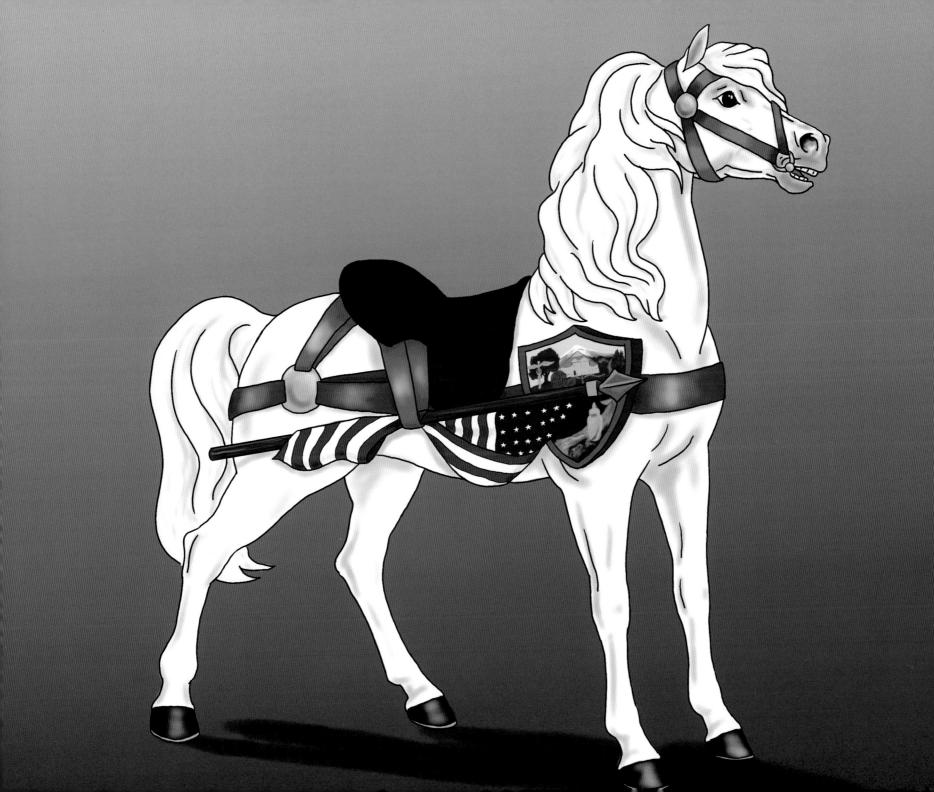

For a few moments all the horses were too stunned to do anything but stand there with their mouths hanging open. Little Joe hadn't heard, and he wasn't tall enough to see. He struggled to squeeze his nose through the long legs of the full-grown horses so he could get in close.

"What did he say? Did he cuss?"

"Worse than that," snorted Abby.

Highland Laddie said, "No wonder he's never talked."

"He's a fraud," hissed Liberty.

"We've been tricked," cried Goldie.

And Brown Beauty said, "This must be someone's idea of a joke!"

Little Joe demanded, "What's wrong? What did he say?"

It was American Flyer who finally said it out loud. "General Patton is a girl!"

"A girl?" exclaimed Little Joe. "He can't be!"

"He is. Listen to the voice," cried Heather. "I was so wrong about him!"

"What a terrible mistake! How could the carvers have made such a blunder? They gave The General a stallion's body and a mare's voice," declared Cloud Walker.

"Talk about an impossible dream," said Rosinante.

"Do you think he'd like to be my mom?" Little Joe asked.

"Get lost, kid," replied Bucky.

Dave interrupted their squabbling. "There was no mistake. It was a woman who came up with the idea of having a carousel in Salem. Her name was Hazel Patton, and The General is her horse."

"Well," snorted Bondo, "coming up with an idea is a lot different from being in charge of something. I refuse to take orders from any silly filly."

"You're a blockhead, Bondo," cried Jazz.

"Yeah, and you're not even a real horse," Bondo yelled back, and the fight started all over again.

Dave walked over to The General, and looking exasperated, he asked, "What should we do?"

The General said, "Let me talk to them." She stepped in between Jazz and Bondo, and when she spoke her voice was firm, but gentle. "Jazz, you're very special. You have been selected to represent all of the zebras in Africa. That's an important job. Where do you think you should stand so that people can admire your beautiful stripes?"

Jazz looked around the circle until he located a spot in the sun. "I think I'd like to work over there," he said.

"That makes sense to me, " said the General.

The minute Jazz climbed up on his new pole it was obvious to everyone it was just where he belonged.

Next The General addressed the paint pony called Sonshine. "You know Sonshine, the Native American people believe that whoever rides a horse with markings like yours will be spiritually protected. That's a huge responsibility. You'll need to be in a spot where your spirit can soar. Do you have any thoughts on where that might be?"

Sonshine nodded thoughtfully. Then without any discussion, he trotted proudly to his place.

Next the General addressed Hero. "You are a strong, dependable draft horse, but I noticed you've been assigned to a spot where you have to push. Is that really what you like to do?"

Hero shook his head. "No, I wasn't designed to do that." He motioned to a spot on the far side of the circular platform. "If I stood there, I think I could easily pull my own weight, and that would make me very happy."

The General smiled. "Good thinking, Hero."

Rain Dancer was the next in line. The General asked, "Rain Dancer, do you know what I appreciate the most about you?"

"I wouldn't have a clue," he sniffed loudly.

"Every living thing needs water. Without it people and animals would die. Flowers wouldn't bloom and trees wouldn't grow. I want to thank you for your abundance of moisture."

"Oh, you're welcome," he cried. "I'm so happy to know I have something good to offer." Tears gushed from his eyes.

And so it went. The General took the time to talk with every horse. One by one they each found something special they could give to the group. Everyone, that is, except for Little Joe, who was standing all alone looking very small and scared. It appeared that all of the spots had been taken. Someone asked if The General might think Little Joe was too small to do anything important. A few of the big horses even questioned if the foal might have to leave the Carousel, and they wondered what would happen to him. Where would he go? Who would take care of him?

Little Joe's knees were shaking. "What about me?" he cried.

The General said, "Follow me, Little Joe," and she wove her way in between two rows of horses until she reached the far outside edge of the platform.

"Little Joe, you're not big enough to be on a pole like the grown up horses."

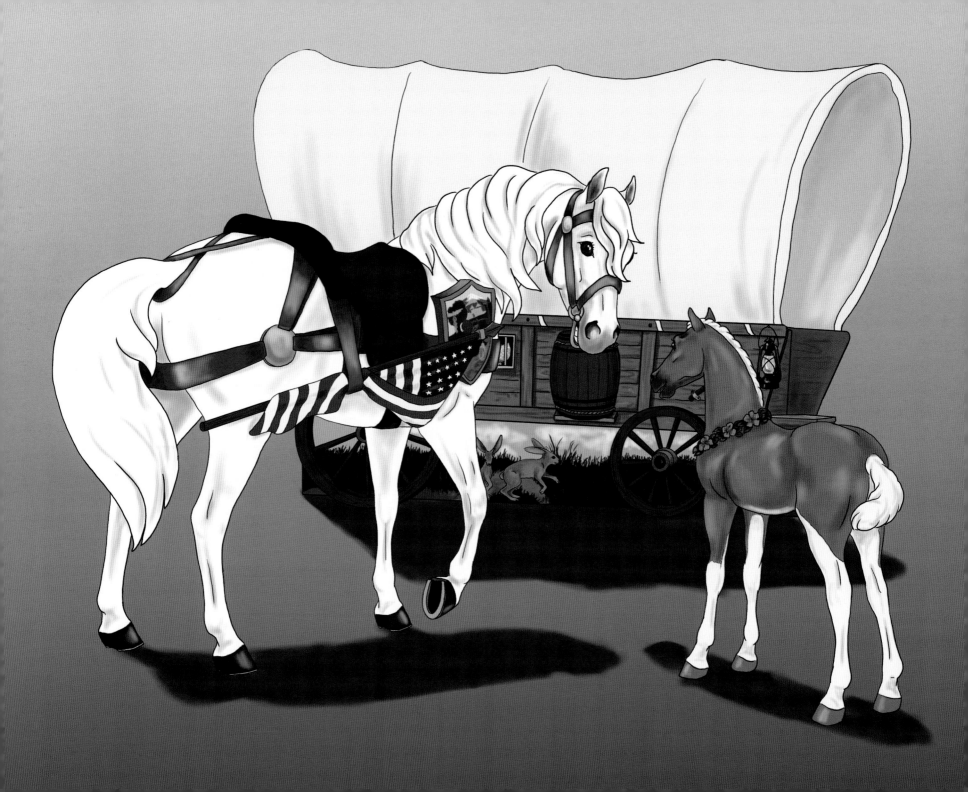

"So there isn't any place for me?" he asked choking on a sob.

"Of course there's a place for you, Little Joe – first place."

The big horses standing close by gasped, then whispers rippled all the way around the Carousel, "The baby gets to be first. The baby gets to be first."
Little Joe was confused. "I didn't think I could do anything, and now you're telling me I get to be first. I don't understand." he said.

The General nudged him gently into a spot by the wagon, then said, "Little Joe, tiny babies come to ride on the Carousel. But think how scary and dangerous it could be for them to be on a big horse that's sailing around, sliding up and down on a tall pole. If you'll stand right here mommies and daddies can sit down on the seat of the wagon and their little ones can take their first Carousel ride safely on your back."

Little Joe stepped into his new place and stood up tall and proud. "I never dreamed I'd have such an important job."

The big horses all nodded and smiled. It made perfect sense – Little Joe was right where he should be.

By the time bedtime rolled around Cloudwalker and two other horses had been taken to the horse hospital to have their wounds sanded and repainted, and the replacement horses had come out of storage to fill their empty spots. Almost everyone was asleep when Dave walked around the Carousel one last time making his final check. "Little Joe, how come you're still awake?"

"I just can't figure it out."

"What?"

"What was The General's secret? Was it that HE was really a SHE?"

"Nope. I don't think it ever crossed The General's mind to wonder whether the job should be done by a mare or a stallion."

"But it couldn't have been the bad words. She didn't say any."

"You're right. That's never been her style."

"Then what was it?"

Dave pulled a handkerchief out of his pocket and rubbed out a smudge on Little Joe's shoulder before replying, "The General knew that the people who carved and painted the horses were wonderful people. They cared so much about the Carousel, that every day they put their hands into the wood, and their hearts into the project. As a matter of fact, they put so much of themselves into it that the horses ended up with some human characteristics."

"Oh, that explains it," replied Little Joe. "People aren't perfect, are they?"

"Far from it. Some of us are opinionated like Magic, others are like Rain Dancer, and cry at the drop of a hat. A few are even ornery like ole' Bucky, who always seems to be looking for some toes to step on or rear ends to kick. The General knows that we all act a little ugly sometimes, but inside we each have something special that makes us different from everyone else. Did you notice how all the horses stopped picking on each other and even started encouraging one another?"

"You're right. They weren't even mad that I got to be first."

"That's because The General helped each one of them find their own talents. And once they knew they were doing something meaningful, they felt proud of themselves and better about everyone else around them."

Little Joe thought hard for a moment, then he said, "It sounds to me like she has a lot of good old-fashioned horse sense."

Dave chuckled a bit, then gave Little Joe a hug. "You're right, she does. And you know what? I think maybe that's The General's secret!"

SALEM'S RIVERFRONT CAROUSEL

In 1996, Hazel Patton visited Missoula, Montana where she saw the first old-world style carousel built in the U.S. since the Great Depression. While impressed with the ornately carved and hand-painted horses, she discovered the real beauty was how the carousel had united that community by combining local history with the creative talents of Missoula's citizens. It has been Hazel's vision and dedication that has brought Salem's Riverfront Carousel to the banks of the Willamette.

Since that time, Salem's Riverfront Carousel project has brought together a diversified group of volunteers, including Dave and Sandy Walker. Together they have directed the creative efforts of hundreds of woodcarvers and painters. Sandy, a talented artist, met with the 43 adopters and designed the horses and symbols that represent each family and business. In addition, she has led the group of artists who have painted the horses and various other carvings on the Carousel. Dave, a master carver, trained most of the woodcarvers and has overseen thousands of hours of loving, but painstaking work.

The vision of Salem's Riverfront Carousel is to touch the hearts, spark the imaginations, and ignite the creative spirits of a broad spectrum of volunteers by creating a work of art that will stand as an historical landmark and an enduring symbol of community pride and cooperation.

All of the volunteers, including artists, carvers, writers, musicians, general contractors, and business specialists, hope you will come visit Salem's Riverfront Carousel. There's something magical about climbing up high on a wooden horse, listening for the organ music to begin, and anticipating the tummy tickles that are inevitable when the Carousel starts to move and the horses take off on their circular flights.

ABOUT THE AUTHOR

After retiring from a career in television advertising in 1998, Elaine Sanchez moved to Salem with her husband, Alex, from Albuquerque, New Mexico. Believing that life is short and the world is large, Elaine and Alex enjoy world travel and spending time with their kids and grandkids.

Elaine has been an active volunteer with the Carousel project, serving on the board of directors and numerous committees. This is the second book Elaine and Janee created together about Salem's Riverfront Carousel. *How Francis Got His Wink* was published in July 2000. All profits from both books are being donated to help fund the project.

ABOUT THE ILLUSTRATOR

Janee Hughes spent 31 years teaching art in middle school. Since retiring she has pursued a freelance art career. She has illustrated magazines, newspapers and catalogs, and has won awards for her equine paintings.

Salem's Riverfront Carousel project combined Janee's greatest interests – art, horses, and carousels. She has been a dedicated volunteer, painting horses and shields and providing illustrations for books and posters.

Janee works in a variety of media, including watercolor, acrylic, and oil as well as digital graphics. This is the second book she has illustrated using her computer.

Janee and her husband, Bill, live east of Salem where they enjoy their horses and dogs.

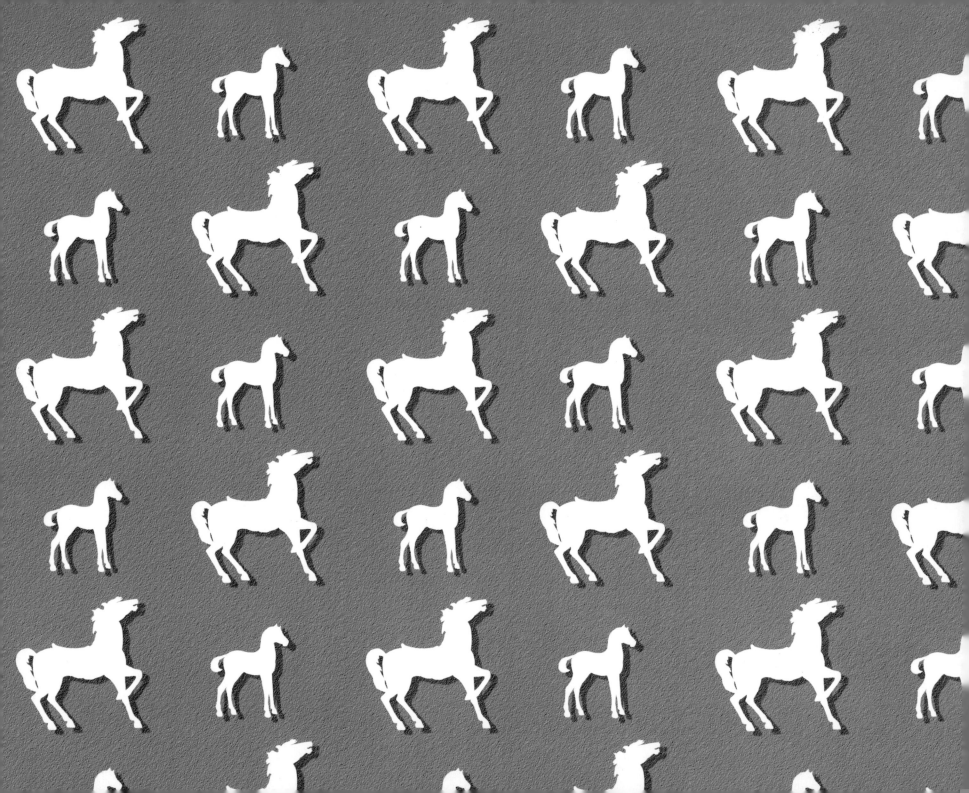